# Gremlins Don't Chew Bubble Gum

by Debbie Dadey
and
Marcia Thornton Jones

illustrated by John Steven Gurney

A
**LITTLE APPLE**
PAPERBACK

## SCHOLASTIC INC.

New York   Toronto   London   Auckland   Sydney

ISBN 0-590-48115-0

Text copyright © 1995 by Marcia Thornton Jones and Debra S. Dadey
Illustrations copyright © 1995 by Scholastic Inc.
All rights reserved. Published by Scholastic Inc.
APPLE PAPERBACKS is a registered trademark of Scholastic Inc.

36 35 34 33 32 31 30 29                                4 5 6 7 8 9/0

Printed in the U.S.A.                                        40

First Scholastic printing, March 1995

Book design by Laurie Williams

*To the members of Writers Ink in Lexington, Kentucky, with special thanks to Alexis, Jerrie, Joel, Mark, Becky, Janice, Tom, and Wendy for helping us find the gremlins in our writing.*
— MTJ and DD

# Contents

# Gremlins Don't Chew Bubble Gum

# 1

## Pop!

Snap! Pop! The lights in the third-grade classroom went out. The only light came from the windows along one wall.

"It's a blackout!" shrieked Liza.

Eddie jumped out of his seat, his curly red hair bouncing. "All right, we get to go home! We can't have school in the dark."

Mrs. Jeepers, their teacher, cleared her throat. "Students, I am sure everything will be fine. Principal Davis will make an announcement about this unfortunate electrical failure."

The students waited and waited. Then they waited some more. But the lights stayed off and there was no announcement. Melody and Liza yawned, and Howie tapped his pencil on his desk.

1

Eddie wiggled and squirmed until he fell out of his seat.

Everybody laughed. Everybody, that is, except Mrs. Jeepers. She touched her green brooch and all the students suddenly got very quiet. Whenever Mrs. Jeepers touched her brooch, they knew they had better shape up . . . or else. Most of the third-graders thought Mrs. Jeepers was a vampire. Even Eddie slid quietly back into his seat.

Carey stuck her hand into the air. "I'd be happy to take a note to the secretary."

"That is an excellent idea," Mrs. Jeepers said as Carey smiled. "But it is Melody's turn to deliver a message."

Mrs. Jeepers quickly jotted a note and handed it to Melody. "Please take this to Miss Kidwell," Mrs. Jeepers said.

"Who?" Melody asked.

"Ms. Moore, the regular secretary, is on her honeymoon," Mrs. Jeepers said. "I met her temporary replacement, Miss

Kidwell, this morning when she brought around the lunch tickets."

Carey stuck her tongue out as Melody walked past her desk and out of the third-grade classroom. Melody looked down the long dark hallway and started to turn around to give the note to Carey, but she didn't want the class to think she was afraid. So she took a deep breath and headed into the shadows. It was so dark she had to feel her way by touching the walls. The only light came from her tiny watch.

She had never noticed before how far the office was from her classroom. The office looked at least one hundred miles away. Every room she passed was dark and inside she could hear teachers reassuring their students.

After slowly walking down the tomb-like hall, Melody finally made it to the office. Principal Davis was staring at the electrical fuse box on the office wall. The tiniest woman Melody had ever seen stood next to him. She was wearing a long lime-green dress that was covered with bright orange flowers. The strange woman's jet-black braids stuck out all over her head and sparkled with streaks of silver.

Melody blinked. When she opened her eyes, the woman was looking at Melody, the hundreds of tiny braids hanging limp at her shoulders. Melody couldn't see a fleck of silver in them.

"Yikes!" Melody said to herself.

"What's that, little lady?" the woman asked.

"Uh, lights!" Melody blurted. "There aren't any lights. My teacher wanted me to give this note to Miss Kidwell."

When the lady nodded, her braids swayed. "That would be me!"

Melody handed the note to Miss Kidwell. On Miss Kidwell's right wrist was a bright silver chain. One lonely charm dangled from the bracelet. It was a lightbulb charm.

Miss Kidwell nodded and chuckled. "Your teacher is right. The lights have gone kaput!"

"They're definitely kaput. What this old building needs is new wiring." Principal Davis grumbled and scratched the shiny top of his bald head. "I wonder if one of these switches will turn the lights back on." Principal Davis reached in the fuse box and punched a button. The radio on the secretary's desk blared to life. Then he punched another button. This time, the electric pencil sharpener started buzzing.

"It must be this one," Principal Davis said as he punched a third button. Suddenly, the bell clanged throughout the halls of Bailey Elementary. Melody clapped her hands over her ears and Miss Kidwell started laughing. Principal Davis quickly punched more buttons, but the bell kept ringing. "I've tried everything I can think of," he yelled over the ringing bell. "This is a very tricky problem."

Miss Kidwell winked at Melody. "It's a good trick, all right. You kids can't work with this racket. It must be your lucky day."

"You don't know my teacher," Melody told her. "Mrs. Jeepers will make us work no matter what. Besides, I really wanted to show my science project video, but I can't do that without electricity."

Miss Kidwell placed her hands on her hips and shook her head. "Tsk, tsk, tsk. No need to frown. The problem is only temporary like me! You need lights, so I'll help."

"But when?" Melody asked. "I'm supposed to show my video after lunch."

"Don't worry about the time." Miss Kidwell tapped Melody's watch. "You won't miss that special science class."

Melody smiled. "Thanks. I can show everyone how I used ten different seeds to attract birds to my yard."

Miss Kidwell nodded. "You must be a very smart girl. Now scoot to class."

Melody stopped at the office door and watched Miss Kidwell wave good-bye. Was it her imagination or were there two charms dangling from Miss Kidwell's bracelet now?

# 2

## Time to Play

When Melody got back to the room, the class was lining up for an early recess.

"Perhaps by the time we get back, the lights will be on," Mrs. Jeepers explained and rubbed her forehead, "and the bell will be silent."

"I hope the lights never come back on," Eddie told Melody, Howie, and Liza when they got outside. They were standing under a big oak tree on the playground.

"Miss Kidwell promised the lights would be on soon," Melody told them.

"I hope so," Liza said. "We can't show our science projects in the dark."

Eddie leaned against the oak tree. "I'd probably get a better grade in the dark," he admitted.

"Wait till you see mine. It's incredible,"

10

Howie told his friends. "It's all about radio waves. My dad helped me with it." Howie's dad was a scientist at FATS, the Federal Aeronautics Technology Station, a nearby research laboratory.

"That's not fair," Eddie complained. "You got special help. I had to make my stupid remote control airplane by myself."

"You're mad because it didn't work," Liza said. "My project's about static electricity. The best part is when your hair stands straight up." She pulled her blonde hair up as high as it would go.

"You look like you stuck your finger in a light socket and got fried," Eddie said.

"That's how the secretary looked," Melody said.

"My aunt says getting married will do that to you," Liza giggled.

Melody shook her head. "I mean the temporary secretary. When I went to the office, her hair was standing straight up and it looked like it had electricity running through it."

Eddie patted Melody on the back. "Maybe she left her electric rollers in too long."

"I'm serious," Melody said. "There's something very strange about her."

"What?" Howie asked.

"I don't know," Melody said. "But I'm going to figure it out."

"Well, while you're figuring, let's play kickball," Eddie suggested. He snatched a ball and raced to the far end of the playground. A few other kids joined them and they quickly chose teams. They played and played until they were out of breath. Then they played some more.

When it was Liza's turn, she rushed toward the big red ball and kicked as hard as she could. Unfortunately, she missed and she fell down in the dirt. "Ow!" Liza said.

Eddie laughed out loud. "Liza can't even kick the ball," he hollered.

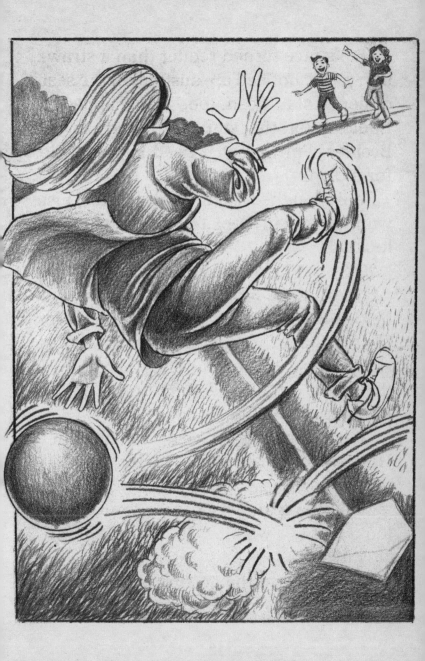

Liza's face turned redder than a straw-berry. She hopped up, dusting off the seat of her pants. "I can, too," she snapped at Eddie. "But the sun was in my eyes. Besides, I'm thirsty. I need to go inside for a drink."

Eddie laughed even harder. "You just want to go in because you can't play kickball."

"Do not," Liza sputtered.

"I'm thirsty, too," Melody interrupted before Eddie could tease Liza anymore. "But we can't go inside yet. The bell is still ringing." The four kids listened to the shrill ringing coming from Bailey Elementary school.

"You think they'd have it fixed by now," Howie said. He looked at Melody. "What time do you have?"

Melody sat down on the ground and looked at her watch. "Oh, no!" she cried. "It's broken."

"That's weird that your watch and the school clocks would break at the same

time," Liza said, stooping beside Melody.

"That's it!" Melody jumped up. "I just realized what's so strange about Miss Kidwell."

"What?" Liza asked.

"Everything she touches gets messed up," Melody explained.

"Just like Liza." Eddie laughed. "She even messes up kickball."

"No, I mean really messed up," Melody said.

"Like your brain," Eddie said. "Nobody

can touch things and make them mess up."

"Unless she's a gremlin," Howie suggested.

"A what?" Melody, Liza, and Eddie asked together.

"A gremlin," Howie said. "My dad told me about them when we were having trouble with my science project. Gremlins are little creatures that mess up mechanical things."

"I mess up mechanical things all the time at my house," Eddie said. "I guess that makes me a gremlin."

"That makes you a walking disaster," Melody said. "But this thing with Miss Kidwell is serious. First, it was the lights, now our watches. What will be next?"

# 3

## Frozen in Time

Howie looked at his friends. "Melody's right. We might be in the middle of a mechanical emergency. I wonder if the rest of the clocks are working."

"I hope not," Eddie said. "Then we could stay outside all day."

"But I don't want to play anymore," Liza whined.

"You're just mad because you missed the ball," Eddie snapped.

Howie ignored Eddie. "Let's go inside and check the clocks."

"And ruin a perfectly good recess?" Eddie asked.

"We can't stay outside forever," Melody pointed out.

Eddie shrugged. "Why not?"

"Because we have to demonstrate our

science projects," Liza reminded him.

Eddie rolled his eyes. "I don't give a hoot about the science projects."

"Don't come, then," Howie said. "We'll find out the truth about Miss Kidwell without you." Howie walked to the building with Melody and Liza close behind.

"Howie ruins all my fun," Eddie complained and raced after them.

Inside the building, the bell echoed in the empty halls and Liza put her hands over her ears to muffle the sound. "This is giving me a headache," she said.

"School always gives me a headache," Eddie griped.

Howie pointed to a clock hanging on the wall. Everyone looked, but nobody said a word.

"Let's check another one to be sure," Liza suggested.

They turned a corner and Melody stopped so fast, Liza bumped into her. Melody stared at another clock. "They're all frozen at 10:28," she said over the

ringing bell. "That's the exact time I was in the office. I noticed because Miss Kidwell tapped my watch."

"She *is* a gremlin," Liza yelped.

"You can't seriously believe a secretary with crazy hair stopped time!" Eddie said. "The lights went off, remember? These clocks use electricity, too."

"Shhh," Howie warned, his fingers to his lips. "I hear something."

"You'd be in trouble if you didn't," Eddie said. "That bell is loud enough to wake a hibernating bear."

Howie shook his head. "I'm not talking about the bell. There's something else."

"It sounds like popcorn popping, only louder," Melody said.

Liza licked her lips. "I wish it was popcorn. I'm hungry."

"It reminds me of the static on my science project radio," Howie said. "I bet it's coming from the office."

"You're crazy," Eddie said. "You're just hearing static from your brain. There's nothing in the office but a substitute secretary."

Howie gave his friend a dirty look. "If you're not going to help, then go back outside. But the rest of us are going to get to the bottom of this."

"Besides," Melody said, "we still need to find out what time it is."

"All right," Eddie mumbled. "I am getting a little hungry. I'd hate to miss lunch."

"Let's go." Howie led the way down the dark hallway, pausing every once in a while to listen to the strange popping noises.

"The noise is coming from everywhere," Liza whimpered.

Melody shook her head. "It's coming from the intercom."

They turned the last corner and stared into the office. There was Miss Kidwell. Her braids shook and they were glowing silver. She was standing at the intercom system, twirling the dials and chewing bubble gum.

"Look at her hair," Melody squeaked. "I told you she had silver streaks."

Eddie squinted. "You're just seeing things."

"Well, if it isn't the scientist," Miss Kidwell said, facing the kids.

"We need to know if it's lunchtime," Eddie blurted. "I'm hungry."

"All the clocks are frozen in time," Melody interrupted. "We've been outside forever."

"Isn't that good?" Miss Kidwell laughed. "A day in the sunshine."

"That's what I said," Eddie told her. "But these goody-two-shoes want to show their science projects."

"Besides, we're tired," Liza said. "You can only chase a ball so long!"

Miss Kidwell laughed again. "Tired of playing? I've never heard of such a thing. But don't worry, it is time for recess to end." Miss Kidwell's bracelet with her two charms made a tinkling sound as she pointed at Melody's watch. Then Miss

Kidwell blew the biggest bubble the kids had ever seen.

"Now, outside before your teacher misses you." Miss Kidwell scooted the kids out into the hall and watched them turn the corner. But the four friends peeked back around the corner and saw Miss Kidwell blow another huge bubble the size of a tennis ball. She climbed up on a step stool and reached her hand out, touching the electrical fuse box. Then she sucked in the bubble with a huge *pop!* Immediately, the lights flickered on and the bell stopped ringing. The kids shivered. For some reason, the sudden silence was worse than the bell. Much worse.

# 4

## Charming

"Did you see her hair?" Melody squealed when they were in the lunchroom. "It was alive!"

Eddie shook his head. "I'm telling you, she was just chewing that big wad of gum too hard."

"It's not right," Liza complained after sipping her chocolate milk. "It's against the rules to chew gum in school."

"At least we know she's not a gremlin," Eddie said.

"What makes you say that?" Melody asked.

"I'm pretty sure that gremlins don't chew bubble gum," Eddie said and took a bite of his cold pizza. Everything was cold because there was no electricity that morning.

"Gum doesn't mean anything, but her charm bracelet does," Melody said.

"What does a bracelet have to do with anything?" Eddie asked.

Melody wiped her mouth with a napkin and spoke slowly. "The first time I saw her, she only had one charm on her bracelet. Now there are three."

"Who cares about jewelry?" Eddie muttered.

"You should care," Melody explained. "Because one of the charms was a light-bulb and another was a clock."

"So?" Eddie said.

Melody rapped her knuckles against Eddie's head. "Hello, anybody in there? Don't you get it?"

Howie, Liza, and Eddie all shook their heads.

Melody rolled her eyes. "You guys would never make it on a game show. I have to tell you everything. Miss Kidwell is a gremlin and every time she messes something up, she gets a new charm."

"Every time I mess something up, I get in trouble." Eddie laughed. "I should have about a million charms by now. I couldn't even carry my bracelet it would be so heavy."

Liza and Howie laughed, but Melody frowned. "You guys aren't taking this seriously. Miss Kidwell is ruining Bailey Elementary."

"Don't get your shorts all ruffled," Eddie said after gulping the last of his milk. "So far we've had a long recess and haven't had to show our science projects. To me, it's been a great day."

"Here comes Mrs. Jeepers," Liza said. "It's time to show our science projects now." Eddie groaned as all the kids lined up behind their teacher.

"I am sorry, students," Mrs. Jeepers said when they were back in their classroom. "Because of the electricity problem, we will only have time for a few science project demonstrations today. We will save the rest for tomorrow."

Howie raised his hand and volunteered. "I'd be happy to go first." Mrs. Jeepers nodded and Howie carried his project to the front of the room.

"My dad explained it to me, but I built this radio all by myself," he said proudly. "Radios work by receiving electromagnetic waves through the air."

Mrs. Jeepers smiled her odd little half-smile, but Eddie raised his hand. "Can't we hear it?" he asked.

"Certainly," Howie said proudly, and with a click he turned a knob. *Squeal! Squeal!*

The entire class covered their ears. "Ouch!" Liza whined. "Turn it off!"

"I don't understand," Howie said. "It worked perfectly last night. It probably just needs tuning." Howie fiddled with the knobs, but the squealing continued. The entire class had their heads on their desks, covering their ears with their arms.

Mrs. Jeepers tapped Howie on the shoulder. "It is a fine project," she said,

"but perhaps you should turn it off."

Howie's shoulders slumped as he turned off the radio and carried it back to his seat. He didn't say a word while Carey and Melody showed their projects.

After school, under the oak tree, Howie kept muttering, "It worked perfectly last night. I just don't understand."

Liza pointed as Miss Kidwell climbed aboard a school bus. "That's strange," Liza said. "She's riding the school bus home."

"I'll tell you what's strange," Melody told her friends. "Remember when we went into the office and Miss Kidwell was playing with the knobs on the intercom?"

"She was trying to figure out how to use it," Howie explained.

"Or she was sabotaging things with knobs," Melody said. "When I looked at her bracelet, there was a new charm on it. And it was a radio!"

# 5

## Dark Ages

"That temporary secretary is causing an electrical emergency," Melody said, leaning against the oak tree.

Eddie laughed. "The only thing temporary around here is your sanity!"

"You have to admit," Liza said, "it's mighty odd the way everything Miss Kidwell touches goes on the blink."

"Like a gremlin," Howie said with a nod.

"Just because your dad mentioned them, you think you're an expert," Eddie blurted. "But what do you really know?"

Howie shrugged. "You have a point. Maybe we are jumping to conclusions."

"But we have to do something," Melody said, "before Miss Kidwell takes Bailey City back to the Dark Ages."

"What would be wrong with that?" Eddie asked, grabbing onto a low branch and climbing into the tree. "If there wasn't any electricity, maybe they'd cancel school forever!"

"And we couldn't have television," Howie reminded him.

"Or CD players," added Liza.

"Or video games," finished Melody.

Eddie slid down the trunk of the tree. "This *is* serious. We have to do something!"

"But first, we need more information," Howie told his friends. "And I know just the place."

"Where?" his three friends asked at once.

"FATS!" Howie told them. "Meet back here in ten minutes with your bikes."

Fifteen minutes later, the kids started the long ride to the Federal Aeronautics Technology Station. FATS was located at the very edge of Bailey City. It took them nearly a half hour just to get there.

They leaned their bikes against the eight-foot-tall wire fence that circled the station.

"I didn't realize it was so far," Liza panted, trying to catch her breath. "It took forever to get here."

"We could've been here in half the time if you had put more power into pedaling," Eddie griped.

"Liza went as fast as she could," Melody interrupted. "And we're here. So stop complaining."

"Fine," Eddie snapped. "But how are we going to get past this fence?"

"No problem." Howie walked up to a small post by the driveway and pushed a big button. Static exploded from a little black speaker perched on top of the post.

"May I help you?" a woman's voice boomed from the box.

"It's Howie Jones. I'm here to see my dad."

The box was quiet for a few seconds before the static continued. "Please follow the drive to the front door."

Slowly the tall gates swung open. As soon as the four friends were inside, the gates shut with a loud clang.

"How can your dad work all locked up like this?" Melody said with a shiver.

"We're locked up every day in school," Eddie mumbled. "And they expect us to work."

"We're not really locked up," Liza said.

Howie ignored Eddie and Liza. "They have to be careful," he told Melody as he led the way toward the sprawling concrete building. "FATS is involved in top-secret experiments."

A pretty woman in a long white lab coat met them at the front door. She glared down her pointy nose at them. "Your father is waiting for you."

Howie rushed his friends down a long hallway to his dad's office. They scooted inside and closed the door. Howie's dad was sitting at a computer, but he stopped typing when the kids came in. He looked just like Howie, only taller, and he wore gold-rimmed glasses that kept sliding down his nose. "What's going on?" he asked.

"We have gremlins," Melody blurted.

Howie's dad smiled. "So, you're having trouble with your science projects, too?"

"Yes," Eddie mumbled. "But that's not why we're here."

"We need information," Howie said before Eddie could say anything else. "You told me about gremlins the other night. We want to know more."

"Gremlins are just a joke." Howie's dad pushed his glasses back on his nose. "People like to kid around when things don't work well."

Melody's eyes got big. "Did you say *kid?*"

"And *well?*" Liza added.

"*Kidwell.*" Howie nodded. "Tell us more, Dad."

Howie's dad smiled again. "Gremlins," he told them, "were first mentioned

during World War I when British planes started having mechanical problems that no one could explain. Small things kept going wrong, almost like someone was playing a joke on the pilots. But it happened so much, there was the fear that the entire Allied Air Force would be grounded."

"What kind of problems did they have?" Eddie asked.

Howie's dad shrugged and pushed his glasses up again. "The lights would go off, alarms went berserk, and the monitors gave wrong information."

"Like shrieking bells?" Melody asked quietly, as if she were afraid to hear the answer, "and clocks telling the wrong time?"

"Why, yes," Howie's dad said. "Those are two of the problems many pilots reported."

Howie nodded. "How did they figure out it was a gremlin?"

"Nobody really knows for sure,"

Howie's dad warned. "But there were consistent reports from pilots about seeing a small creature with wild hair messing with the equipment during flights."

"Did they ever catch her?" Liza asked.

Howie's dad shook his head and smiled. "I suppose that mischievous creature decided to go bother someone else with pranks because nobody ever found her."

Melody let out a little groan. "I think we found her! And she's working at Bailey Elementary!"

# 6

## Attack Plane

The next morning Eddie was still trying to get his science experiment to work. Eddie and Melody were under the oak tree looking at it when Miss Kidwell came up behind them.

"Lovely morning, isn't it?" Miss Kidwell said, chewing a big wad of bubble gum.

Melody nodded, but Eddie frowned. "It might be okay if I could get this remote control plane to work."

"What's wrong with it?" Miss Kidwell asked.

Eddie held up the bright blue plane for her to see: "It's dead," he said.

"I've always been partial to blue planes myself," she said, touching it with her hand. Before she let go, she blew a big pink bubble and popped it. "Well, we'd

40

better get to school before we're late,"
Miss Kidwell said.

"Don't worry," Melody told Eddie.
"Howie's radio didn't work, either." Eddie
sighed and stuffed the plane into his
backpack.

Inside the classroom Eddie was the first
to demonstrate his project. Slowly, he
carried his plane to the front of the room.

"What a lovely project," Mrs. Jeepers
said and smiled her half-smile at Eddie.

"It doesn't work, though," Eddie mumbled.

"Why don't you try it?" Howie suggested. Mrs. Jeepers nodded. Eddie put the plane on the floor and pulled a knob on his controller.

To Eddie's surprise, the plane flew into the air and zoomed around the room. "It's working!" Eddie screamed, jumping up and down.

The plane made two passes around the room near the ceiling and then zoomed lower. It flew close to Melody's head and zipped right past Howie. Liza screamed when it zipped a circle around her head, and Carey fell off her chair when it aimed right at her.

"Turn it off!" Liza screamed as the plane chased her around the room.

Eddie jiggled the dials on his controller back and forth, but nothing happened. "I'm trying," he told Liza, "but it won't turn off!"

The plane roared up to the ceiling, did

a flip, and then dive-bombed right toward Mrs. Jeepers. "Oh, no!" Eddie yelled and leaped into the air. He caught the plane right before it landed on Mrs. Jeepers' head.

The whole class sighed and Mrs. Jeepers rubbed her green brooch. "Eddie, I would like you to take a time-out in the hall," she said.

"But, it wasn't my fault . . ." Eddie tried to explain.

Mrs. Jeepers shook her head and pointed to the hallway. Eddie knew there was no use in arguing. He grabbed his plane and headed out the door.

# 7

## Musical Bus

After school Eddie met Melody, Howie, and Liza under the shade of the oak tree. Eddie was still mad about his science project. "It wasn't my fault," Eddie snapped before they could say a word. "It wouldn't even work last night. Then it almost attacks Mrs. Jeepers. I don't understand!"

"I do," Melody said softly.

Eddie glared at Melody. "You don't know anything!"

"I know Miss Kidwell was very interested in your plane this morning," Melody told him.

"She said that she liked blue planes," Liza reminded him. "Then she touched it."

"Just as she blew a huge bubble," Howie added.

Melody snapped her fingers. "I bet she fixes things when she blows a bubble."

"You can't believe she made my plane fly," Eddie said. "After all, you told me gremlins mess things up."

"If they can mess them up, then they can probably fix them, too," Howie reasoned. "Besides, Dad said they like to play tricks."

Melody giggled. "I think your attack plane was a funny trick."

Eddie was ready to make Melody stop laughing, but a loud noise stopped him. At the bus stop, they saw Mrs. Gurney, the bus driver, scratching her head and talking to Principal Davis. "I don't understand. It was running fine this morning." She kicked a tire, while the kids on the bus clapped and hollered.

"Maybe it's out of gas," Principal Davis told her.

Mrs. Gurney glared at Principal Davis.

"I've been driving school buses for twelve years. It's not out of gas. If you don't believe me, try it yourself." Mrs. Gurney tossed the keys to Principal Davis and watched him climb into the driver's seat. When he turned the key, the engine roared to life. But that's not all that happened.

The bus's horn blasted so loud, Liza had to cover her ears. The kids on the bus laughed as the horn honked out the tune of "Rain, Rain, Go Away."

Principal Davis held his hands in the air. "Crazy horn. It must be stuck. I guess you'll have to drive it this way."

"Are you nuts?" Mrs. Gurney bellowed. "I can't drive through town with the horn blasting like that!"

"You have to get these kids home. They live too far away to walk," Principal Davis told her. "So you have to drive the bus."

Just then, the bus switched songs, blaring out "The Itsy, Bitsy Spider." The kids on the bus screamed and clapped with the song. Mrs. Gurney put her hand on her forehead. "I have a feeling it will take me a long, long time to get rid of this headache."

As the bus drove down the street, Melody, Liza, Howie, and Eddie heard "Mary Had a Little Lamb" echoing across Bailey City. They heard something else, too. Something that sent chills down their backs.

# 8

# A Pretty Good Trick

The four kids turned to see Miss Kidwell on the school steps. She was singing "Mary Had a Little Lamb." When she saw the kids looking at her, she popped a bubble and laughed. The honking stopped and she waved to them.

Melody gasped. "She made the music stop!"

"If you call that music," Howie said.

"You guys are crazy," Eddie said, rolling his eyes. "I've had some pretty tough bubble gum before, but I've never had any tough enough to make magic."

"Shh," Liza said. "Here she comes."

Miss Kidwell laughed as she walked up to the children. "That bus honking was a pretty good trick, don't you think? I've always liked music."

Liza looked at Miss Kidwell for a minute before she asked, "Why didn't you ride the bus home today?"

"That's right," Melody said. "You rode it yesterday."

Miss Kidwell smiled. "You are such smart children to notice. Today, I'm walking to the public library for some exercise. So I'd better be on my way!" Miss Kidwell waved good-bye and walked away from the kids.

Melody watched until Miss Kidwell went around the corner of the school. Then Melody looked at her friends. "Did you see it?" she asked.

"See what?" Eddie asked.

"Her charm bracelet, of course!" Melody shrieked. "She has five charms now!"

"So?" Liza said. "Maybe she got paid and bought some more."

"But doesn't it seem strange that she bought a radio, a plane, and a bus?" Melody asked.

Howie's face went pale. "Those are the

things that went wrong or got fixed."

Melody nodded her head. "Exactly. And if we don't do something soon, there's no telling what might happen next."

Eddie laughed. "You need to learn to relax. Maybe you should try yoga. Miss Kidwell is not a gremlin and nothing really bad has happened."

"What about your plane attacking the class?" Howie asked.

Eddie laughed. "I have to admit that was funny, even if I did get in trouble."

Liza giggled. "Eddie's right. Maybe the bus and electricity were just accidents."

"Don't forget about Howie's radio and Eddie's plane," Melody reminded them. "I just hope the secretary gets back from her honeymoon before Bailey Elementary ends up a disaster area!"

# 9

## Bailey Spies

"I know what to do," Howie said. "Let's go!"

"Wait a minute!" Eddie grabbed Howie's jacket and pulled him back under the shade of the big oak tree. "Go where?"

"To the library," Howie sputtered. "Where else?"

"The library!" Eddie yelled. "I'd rather eat worms than go there. I want to play soccer."

Howie rolled his eyes at Eddie. "The Bailey library has all the answers we need. Besides the books, we can do a little spying on Miss Kidwell."

"Spying!" Liza gasped.

"Now you're talking." Eddie grinned. "Spying is almost as fun as soccer."

Melody ignored Eddie. "What can we find out from watching Miss Kidwell in the library?" she asked.

Howie walked away, but he answered Melody over his shoulder. "I don't know. But we have to do something, and the only thing I can think of is to get some facts."

Howie's friends followed him away from the school, down Forest Lane, and into the quiet shadows of the Bailey City library.

"I want to be the spy!" Eddie said.

"Shhh!" Melody warned. "You know how grumpy Mr. Cooper gets about noise."

Just then, Mr. Cooper walked up to the four Bailey students. His footsteps echoed on the wooden floors. He put his hands on his hips and squinted his eyes. "I am in no mood for mischief," he warned. "I don't want to hear any complaints about you kids."

"Yes, Mr. Cooper," Howie said politely.

"We won't cause any trouble," Liza said.

"Humph, I hope not," Mr. Cooper muttered before walking away.

The kids weaved up and down aisles of books until they reached the section filled with encyclopedias and dictionaries. Howie looked at his friends. "Spread out and find Miss Kidwell while I look up information about gremlins."

"What do we do if we see her?" Liza asked.

"Try to see what books she's looking at," Howie suggested.

Liza and Melody nodded, but Eddie groaned. "I've never heard of spies reading books before."

Howie shrugged and started searching the shelves. Melody, Liza, and Eddie disappeared down another aisle. They hadn't gone far when they spotted Miss Kidwell. Her black-and-silver braids bounced as she chewed a huge wad of gum. She was concentrating on a big blue book.

"Can you see the title?" Melody whispered.

Liza and Eddie shook their heads. "I'll find out," Eddie whispered and sneaked down the aisle. He crouched low and maneuvered close to Miss Kidwell. Liza covered her eyes and Melody held her breath. But Miss Kidwell was too busy reading to notice Eddie's curly head peering up at her from the other side of the bookshelf. Then his head disappeared and soon Eddie was standing next to Melody and Liza. "I told you I'd make a good spy," he said with a grin.

"What was her book about?" Melody asked.

Eddie shrugged. "She's reading about the Federal Aeronautics Technology Station."

"That's odd," Liza said. "Why would she want to know about FATS?"

"I don't know," Melody said slowly.

"But I think we should tell Howie."

Howie was sitting at a long table with a huge book in front of him. "Here's the truth about gremlins!" Howie said as his friends walked up.

"Why don't you check that book out?" Eddie suggested. "That way we could still play soccer for a while."

"I tried to," Howie told him. "But all the library computers crashed. No one can check out a book anywhere in Bailey City."

Just then, laughter sounded from behind them. "Now why would you need a book about gremlins?" Miss Kidwell asked.

Slowly, the kids turned to see Miss Kidwell. The first thing they noticed was the shiny new charm dangling from her bracelet. And it was a computer!

# 10

## Invaded

The next morning, Howie kicked a clod of mud and threw his backpack on the ground near the trunk of the giant oak tree.

"What's wrong with you?" Melody asked. "You look like you haven't slept all night."

"I haven't," Howie snapped. "FATS was invaded!"

"When? How? Why?" his friends asked.

"It happened just after dark," Howie explained. "But nobody can figure out how or why!"

"Then how do you know it was invaded?" Eddie asked.

"Because every computer, every light, and every piece of machinery just quit working . . . all at the same time!" Howie told them.

"Wait a minute," Melody gasped. "I know what happened."

Howie scowled. "Famous scientists can't explain it. How can you?"

"Easy," Melody told him. "We weren't the only ones at the library, remember. We forgot to tell you what we found out about Miss Kidwell."

"Tell me now," Howie said seriously. "The safety of FATS and Bailey City may depend on what you know."

"Let me tell," Eddie said. "After all, I was the one who found it out."

"What was it?" Howie asked.

Eddie stood tall. "I had to use my best spy moves," he said. "I sneaked around the shelves and looked straight at Miss Kidwell's book."

"Tell me!" Howie shouted.

Eddie crossed his arms and said, "Her book was *Federal Aeronautics Technology Station: A Public Guide*."

"That does it!" Howie yelled. "First, it was Bailey Elementary. And then the library. Now, it's FATS. The next thing you know, the White House will be shut down all because of a tricky gremlin."

"But what can we do about it?" Liza asked.

"There's only one thing to do," Howie said with a shaky voice. "And I think I know just what it is."

"What?" Eddie asked.

"If we can find the right good luck charm, we can get rid of Miss Kidwell," Howie told them.

Melody nodded. "All we need is something lucky to help us get rid of our bad luck."

"What's the luckiest thing you own?" Howie asked.

"My soccer underwear!" Eddie shouted. "I haven't washed them all season and we haven't lost a game yet."

"That's because you stink the other teams clear to Sheldon City." Melody laughed.

"I have a horseshoe that my dad told me was lucky," Liza said.

"What about the number seven?" Melody said. "That one is supposed to be lucky."

Howie nodded and checked his glow-in-the-dark watch. "Good idea, and I have a wishbone that I've been saving. It's bound to be good luck. If we hurry, we can get the charms and be back before school starts."

"And if we're really *lucky*," Eddie said, "one of these will get rid of Miss Kidwell and our gremlin troubles will be over."

# 11

## Good Luck

In ten minutes the kids were back under the oak tree with their good luck charms stashed in their backpacks. "How are we going to get all this stuff to Miss Kidwell?" Liza asked.

"No problem," Eddie said. "I'll fly my plane around the room and Mrs. Jeepers will send me to the office. I can dump everything on Miss Kidwell's desk."

Howie shook his head. "We have to sneak in without her knowing it."

"We can each ask to go to the bathroom," Melody suggested.

"Good idea," Howie said. "We'll have to go one at a time. And be careful! There's no telling what Miss Kidwell might do if she finds out our plan."

Melody, Eddie, and Liza grabbed their

backpacks and followed Howie into the school.

At eight-thirty, Howie asked to go to the bathroom. When he got to the office, Miss Kidwell had her back to him. While she was busy pouring a cup of coffee, Howie dropped his wishbone into her pencil cup.

He winked at his friends when he sat back down at his desk. Fifteen minutes later Melody asked to go to the bathroom. Mrs. Jeepers looked at her strangely, but let her go. As soon as Melody was out in

the hall, she pulled a paper out of her pocket. Inside the paper was a green magnetic seven that she'd grabbed off her refrigerator door.

Melody peeked into the office and saw Miss Kidwell answering the phone. Melody held her breath and slipped the seven onto the inside of the office door. Quickly, she ran back into the room and made a thumbs-up sign to her friends.

Liza took a deep breath and patted her sweater where the horseshoe was hidden. "Mrs. Jeepers, may I be excused?" she asked.

Mrs. Jeepers touched the green brooch at her neck. "The bathroom certainly is a popular place this morning. Do you really need to go?"

Liza felt the horseshoe in her pocket and nodded. "It is an emergency," she said.

"Very well, then," Mrs. Jeepers said before turning to write math problems on the blackboard.

Liza was gone almost ten minutes before returning to the classroom.

"Did you do it?" Eddie whispered.

"Yes," Liza said. "I put the horseshoe in her desk."

Eddie raised his hand. "Mrs. Jeepers, may I go to the bathroom?" he asked.

Mrs. Jeepers put her hands on her hips and flashed her green eyes at Eddie. "This bathroom epidemic has to stop. Try to wait until after computer time."

"Yes, ma'am," Eddie said politely. Then under his breath he whispered to Howie, "I didn't want to give away my lucky underwear anyway."

In a few minutes, the class lined up for computers. Working in the school's brand-new computer lab was a treat for the kids. There was a shiny computer for each student. No one gave a thought to gremlins or good luck charms as they worked at their computers.

"All right!" Eddie cheered after a while. "I've almost captured all of Planet Zeon.

If I get three more math problems right, I'll be ruler of the universe!"

But Eddie didn't get the chance. With just one more problem to go, every computer suddenly went black.

"*No!*" Eddie shrieked. "What happened?"

"It must be a bug in the system," Howie explained.

Melody nodded. "A very big bug. And her name is Miss Kidwell."

Liza looked ready to cry. "Our good luck charms didn't work. What are we going to do?"

"This has gone too far," Eddie said, staring at his dark computer screen. "Something has to be done and I know just what it is."

# 12

## In the Clover

"Bring your backpacks outside," Eddie told his friends at recess time.

"What for?" Howie asked.

"I'll explain outside," Eddie said. All four kids carried their backpacks to their meeting place under the oak tree.

"What are we going to do?" Liza asked.

"We're going to good luck Miss Kidwell right out of Bailey City," Eddie told them.

"But we don't have any more good luck charms," Liza whined.

"Yes, we do," Eddie said.

"Where?" his friends asked together.

"You're standing in it," Eddie said. The kids looked at their feet. They were standing in a huge bed of clover.

"Clover!" Melody shouted. "Four-leaf clovers are really lucky."

"Exactly!" Eddie smiled. "I don't know why I didn't think of it before."

"Let's start looking," Howie said, dropping to the ground.

Eddie shook his head. "We don't have time. Just fill your backpacks with as much clover as you can."

"There are bound to be four-leaf clovers in here somewhere," Liza said.

"Hopefully enough to help us save Bailey Elementary," Melody agreed.

Howie started ripping up clovers and stuffing them into his pack. "What are you waiting for?" he shouted. "Let's hurry!"

By the time recess was over, their packs were full of clovers. When the bell rang, instead of going straight to their room, the kids took a detour to the office.

"Now what are we going to do?" Howie asked as they crouched outside the office. They could see Miss Kidwell sitting at the secretary's desk, counting milk money.

"Follow me," Eddie said. He strutted into the office with the backpack securely on his back. His friends came after him.

"We have to sit in the office for a while," Eddie announced to Miss Kidwell. "I guess we've been bad."

Miss Kidwell smiled and chewed her gum. "You don't look bad to me, but sit there." She pointed to some chairs by the door.

The four kids sat stiffly with their packs still on their backs. Melody watched as the seconds ticked by on the office clock.

"We'd better get to our room before Mrs. Jeepers comes looking for us," Liza whispered.

"Be patient," Eddie whispered back. The kids watched the clock and then Miss Kidwell.

"Eddie," Howie said. "Maybe we had better get back . . ."

"Look," Melody hissed. The kids looked at Miss Kidwell. Her braids were hanging limp about her head and she was rubbing her forehead. Finally, she laid her head on the desk.

"Are you all right?" Liza asked Miss Kidwell.

Miss Kidwell shook her head. "No, I have a terrible headache. I think I'd better go home right away." With that, Miss Kidwell rushed out of the office.

Eddie jumped out of his seat and held his backpack over his head. "We did it!" he shouted.

"You can't be sure," Melody warned.

"I'm sure," Eddie said. "I feel lucky."

# 13

## Feeling Lucky

The next day all four kids were feeling lucky when they saw their regular secretary, Ms. Moore, sitting at her desk. Scattered all over the office floor were bubble gum wrappers.

"Welcome back," Liza said politely, giving her some flowers. "We really missed you."

Ms. Moore smiled. "Why, thank you. Although I'm sure Miss Kidwell took very good care of you."

"Don't worry," Eddie said. "We'd rather have *you* any day."

"Where did you go on your honeymoon?" Melody asked.

"We went to England. It was fun. We even got to see the Queen!" Ms. Moore

put her flowers in a vase as Principal Davis walked into the office.

"England?" Principal Davis said. "That's where Miss Kidwell went. She's going there to take flying lessons."

"That figures," Eddie muttered.

"What did you say?" Principal Davis asked.

"Oh, nothing," Eddie said quickly. "I was just wondering what Ms. Moore's married name is."

Ms. Moore smiled. "My new name is Lucky, Mrs. Lucky." The secretary didn't say anything else. She just blew a huge bubble and popped it right in front of the kids.

"Oh, no!" Eddie cried. "Not again!"

**Debbie Dadey and Marcia Thornton Jones** have fun writing stories together. When they both worked at an elementary school in Lexington, Kentucky, Debbie was the school librarian and Marcia was a teacher. During their lunch break in the school cafeteria, they came up with the idea of the Bailey School kids.

Recently Debbie and her family moved to Plano, Texas. Marcia and her husband still live in Kentucky where she continues to teach. How do these authors still write together? They talk on the phone and use computers and fax machines!

JUNIOR        J86607

JF
Dad        Dadey, Debbie

Gremlins don't chew bubble
gum